DON'T GET DIRTY GERTY

For Jenny with love – ED

For Rich – LC

Created exclusively for World International Limited by Bloomsbury Publishing Plc
First published in Great Britain in 1997 by World International Limited, Deanway
Technology Centre, Wilmslow Road, Handforth, Cheshire SK9 3FB

ISBN 0 7498 3091 3

Printed by Bath Press, Great Britain

10 9 8 7 6 5 4 3 2 1

Little Readers

DON'T GET DIRTY GERTY

Elizabeth Dale

Pictures by Louise Comfort

World International Limited

Gerty was very excited. She was going to Jenny's party that afternoon. On the way, she and her mum were picking up all her friends.

At last it was time to put on her new dress.

She looked so pretty, so clean.
In fact, quite unlike Gerty at all!
"Don't get dirty, Gerty!" cried her mum
as they left.
Gerty slammed the door so hard, the
whole house shook!

Don't get dirty, Gerty!

While Mum waited in the car, Gerty called for James. He was cleaning his teeth, which took a very long time!

"Have some slime juice while you wait, Gerty," said James's mum.

Just time for a quick drink!

Gerty held the can well away from her when she opened it.

Next, they went to pick up Harry.

Harry was helping his mum mix a chocolate sludge cake.

Gerty didn't touch the mixture, but she bumped into the table, sending the bowl flying!

Then they arrived at Mandy's house.

Mandy and her mum were sharing a plate of crunchy ants.

Some ants crawled up Gerty's leg. She jumped
up and down and crashed into Mandy.

After that they went to collect Simon.

Simon was snoozing in a hammock.

She shook the hammock to wake him up.

Then they went to pick up Tommy.

Tommy was painting the bird table.

Gerty didn't touch the wet paint, but she knocked over the paint-pot.

The last friend to collect was Susie.

Susie's mum was watering the garden.

Gerty didn't realise she was standing on the hose pipe.

At 4 o'clock they all arrived at the party. "Right on time!" said Gerty. "And I didn't even get dirty, Mum."

"No! But look at your friends," said Gerty's mum.

"Hello! I'm glad you could all come!" cried Jenny's mum. "And how clever of you to wear your scruffy clothes . . .